STUART'S CAPE

BY SARA PENNYPACKER

ILLUSTRATED BY MARTIN MATJE

ORCHARD BOOKS

AN IMPRINT OF SCHOLASTIC INC.

NEW YORK

LIBRARY OF CONGRESS CATALOGING-IN-PUBLICATION DATA

Pennypacker, Sara, 1951 - .
Stuart's Cape / by Sara Pennypacker;
illustrated by Martin Matje. — 1 st ed.   p.   cm.
Summary: Bored because there is nothing to do in
the house to which his family has just moved and
worried about starting third grade in a new school,
Stuart makes a magical cape out of his uncle's ties
and has a series of adventures.

ISBN 0-439-30180-7
[1. Moving, Household — Fiction. 2. Worry —
Fiction. 3. First day of school — Fiction. 4. Junk —
Fiction.] I. Matje, Martin, ill. II. Title.
PZ7.P3856 St 2002   [Fic] — dc21   2001037480

10 9 8 7 6 5 4 3   03 04 05 06

Printed in the United States of America   23
First edition, October 2002

The text type was set in 12-pt. Sabon.
Title type was handlettered by Martin Matje.
Display type was set in Bad Cabbage ICG.
Book design by Marijka Kostiw

For Stuart, of course.
—S. P.

To my mother, who gave me my cape.
—M. M.

STUART MAKES A CAPE

"I want to have an adventure," Stuart moaned for the third time. He mushed his face against the rainy window and squinted. This made the world look smeary. It was fun, but not fun enough.

"I don't have anyone to play with. I can't build anything because all my stuff is gone. I've played horses and dinosaurs and gorillas all morning. Now I want to do something different."

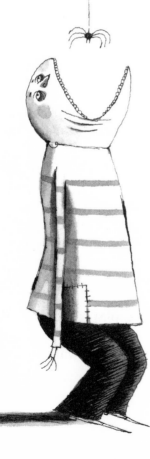

"School starts in a few days," his mother reminded him. "That will be something different."

Stuart had not forgotten this. He had been worrying all week.

Stuart and his family had just moved to Punbury, so he had a lot to worry about. What if there were man-eating spiders in his new bed-room closet? Or, a man eating spiders? What if he got lost? Worst of all, he would be in a new school for third grade. Hundreds of things could go wrong. What if he couldn't find the bathroom? What if he *could* find the bathroom, but he got locked inside? What if no one wanted to be his friend?

Stuart was very good at worrying. He was not so good at waiting.

"Anyway," he sighed, "in a few days is *in a few days*. I want an adventure *now*." He slid down to the floor, next to his cat, to think.

"I wish I were Whizzer the Space Boy," he said to One-Tooth. "I would put on my cape and save a planet. I wish I were Power Tool Man, or Rubberlegs Roger. I would put on my cape and . . . "

Stuart smacked his head and jumped up. "*Of*

course!" he shouted. "Adventures only happen to people with *capes*!"

"Nonsense," said his mother. "People can have adventures in dresses, or nice, warm sweaters."

"In business suits or pajamas," added his father.

"Nope," said Stuart, shaking his head. "The cape is the thing. It must be a rule. I can't even think of one person who ever had an adventure without one. Can you?"

Stuart's mother scrunched her eyes down, thinking hard. His father scratched his chin, thinking hard. Aunt Bubbles tugged her braids, thinking hard. Three lemons fell out. "Oh, good!" she cried. "I was wondering where I packed those."

Aunt Bubbles went into the kitchen to make lemonade. Stuart's parents followed her to make sure nothing exploded. One-Tooth followed them all to see if tuna fish were involved.

Stuart, Stuart said to himself, *you need a cape.*

The hall was full of boxes from moving. None of them was his, though.

Stuart had packed up his best stuff and left it outside for the moving van. But the trash collector had taken it instead! His extremely valuable things, mistaken for trash! A mannequin arm, an oven door, a dead Christmas tree. A cracked toilet seat, a box of bent coat hangers, false teeth . . . wonderful stuff. It had taken him years to collect it.

Stuart poked around in the boxes. No capes. Just some junk his family was throwing out.

A bunch of old ties. A rusty stapler. One purple sock.

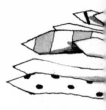

"Hmmm . . ." said Stuart.

One by one, side by side, very carefully, Stuart stapled the ties together. One hundred ties made a wonderful cape! Heavy and smooth and long. Inside, he stapled the purple sock for a secret pocket.

Stuart put the cape on. Things felt different right away.

Very different.

Stuart ran to the hall mirror. He threw his shoulders back and puffed up his chest. He stretched his mouth

wide, but not in a smile. He twisted around so he was looking (boldly) over one shoulder. In this position it was hard to see himself in the mirror. He had to slide his eyeballs around to the edges of his eyes. But it was worth it.

Because there in the mirror was someone who was sure to have adventures. There in the mirror was —

Just then the doorbell rang.

Well, he would think up a name later.

PLAYING STUART

Stuart ran to answer the doorbell. On the doorstep stood a dinosaur, a horse, and a gorilla. Dripping wet.

"Hello," said Stuart, in his most normal voice. "Come on in."

He knew one thing about people who wore capes: They never acted surprised. Even if they went zinging around the solar system, like Whizzer the Space Boy. Even if their arms turned into drills, like Power Tool

Man. Even if they could bounce over parking lots, like Rubberlegs Roger. From now on, no matter what happened, Stuart would not act surprised.

One-Tooth did not care about not acting surprised.

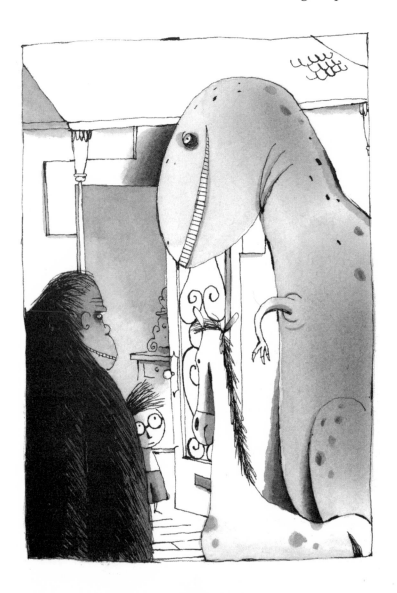

Her eyes bulged out like Ping-Pong balls. Her fur stood up like flames. She tore up the curtains and glared down at the animals.

The visitors did not look happy, either.

"You have been playing animals again. And you do it all wrong," said the dinosaur. "All that crashing around."

"All that trotting and jumping," added the horse.

"All that swinging from branches," grumbled the gorilla. "It's ridiculous. We don't do those things at all."

"What do you do?" asked Stuart, greatly interested.

"Well, we eat," said the gorilla.

"Yes, we eat," said the horse. "And we stand."

"We eat and we stand," said the dinosaur. "And we sleep!" He leaned back into the sofa. "It's very hard to get it right."

"Besides," snorted the horse, "It's rude. We don't pretend to be you."

"You could," Stuart said. "You could play Stuart. I wouldn't mind."

The animals looked at each other. "How would we play it? What do you do?"

"Follow me." Stuart led the animals to his bedroom. "First, I wake up."

"Let me try," said the dinosaur. He jumped onto Stuart's bed.

"I, Stuart, am awake!" cried the dinosaur. "This is a good game so far."

"Stuart!" called his mother from the kitchen. "Are you jumping on your bed again?"

"Of course not!" Stuart called back.

He pointed to his closet. "I get dressed next. I have to watch out for man-eating spiders."

The horse went in and stomped around for a while. He came out sort-of dressed. "Do I look like you?" he asked.

"Sometimes," said Stuart.

"Stuart!" cried Aunt Bubbles. "Are you stomping around in your closet again?"

"I wasn't even *in* my closet!" Stuart answered.

He showed the animals the bathroom. "Next, I get cleaned up."

The gorilla got the idea right away. He turned on the water. He unrolled the toilet paper and squirted toothpaste all over the floor. "Like this?" he asked.

CRASH!!!

"Yep," said Stuart. "Exactly."

"Stuart!" yelled his father. "Are you playing in the bathroom again?"

"Oh, no," Stuart yelled back. "Not me!"

"Playing Stuart gets pretty hard now," he told the animals, going back into the living room. "Every day I have to figure out what to do. School starts soon. When there's no school, I like to play with my friends. Except I haven't made any. Or I build things. Except all my stuff is gone." Stuart heaved a deep sigh of sadness. "Anyway, it's raining today."

"And you eat when it's raining?" asked the horse hopefully.

"I play inside. Games like . . ." Stuart paused to think of an easy one. "Hide-and-seek! I'll teach you. You all hide, and I'll close my eyes. Then I'll find you."

The animals scrambled to hide.

"Stuart!" shouted his family. "What is going on? It sounds like a herd of wild animals in there!"

"Don't worry!" Stuart answered. "There are only three animals here. And they're not *too* wild."

The animals had not hidden very well. But it was their first time, so Stuart pretended he could not find them.

Just then his family came running out of the kitchen. "What do you mean, *three animals?*" they cried. "We don't see any animals!"

"Of course not," said Stuart. He winked. "They are hiding."

"Oh," Stuart's family winked back. "We under-stand."

"They came over because of my cape," Stuart explained. "It's magic."

"Of *course* it is," Stuart's family smiled. "And now we are going to pay some magic bills."

"It was fun playing Stuart," said the animals when

Stuart found them. "But not as much fun as eating. What have you got to eat?"

Aunt Bubbles worked in a bakery. Every day she brought home the leftovers. Stuart found apple pie and bagels and chocolate chip cookies. The animals ate nearly everything in the house. Stuart himself was very hungry. He ate an entire angel food cake.

"Very good," said the animals. "Quite tasty." Then they wiped their mouths with their tails.

Stuart wiped the cake crumbs from his mouth with his new cape.

"Well, good night," said his new friends. "If you get bored again, you may play animals."

"Thanks," said Stuart. He looked down at his new cape and smiled. "But I don't think I'll be getting bored again."

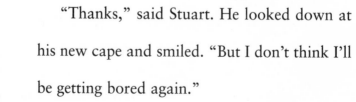

STUART FLIES

Stuart woke up on the ceiling. "Good," he said, remembering not to act surprised. "I can fly."

He flapped his cape and zoomed around his bedroom, getting the hang of it. Then he flew into the kitchen.

"I can fly today!" he cried to his family. "I'm going to have an adventure every day now that I have a cape."

Stuart's father was watching TV. "Quiet!" he said. "It's time for the banking news."

Stuart's mother was reading the paper. "Hush!" she said. "There is a big sale at the E-Z Mart. One toothbrush for the price of two!"

Aunt Bubbles was coloring. "Shhhh!" she said. "I'm trying to draw cake. Eat your breakfast."

Stuart pulled himself down the refrigerator and

LOST
angel food cake
~~big~~ reward
HUGE

along the counter. He grabbed the table. His legs floated in the air. "May I please have some tape?" he asked.

Aunt Bubbles didn't look up from her poster. She gave Stuart the tape. Stuart rolled it into big, sticky balls. He stuck them onto the back of his cape. Now he could sit.

"I guess my cape is magic," Stuart tried again. "I can fly."

"Don't be silly," said his mother. "People can't fly."

"That's impossible!" said his father. "People can't fly."

"It's very hard to draw cake!" said Aunt Bubbles. "Especially when people are talking! Now go outside and play."

"Okay," Stuart sighed. "But I don't think that's such a good idea."

Stuart peeled off the tape balls. Up he rose, like a balloon. He flew to the door. "Good-bye!" he called.

sky, pretending he was a bolt of lightning. Stuart was so busy he forgot to feel lonely. He could do anything.

Except come down.

Some crows flew by.

"Good morning," Stuart said. "Fine day for flying."

And it was. The air was as soft and cool as whipped cream. Down below, the houses looked like chocolate chips in a little cookie town.

But it was a fine day for worrying, too.

Stuart looked down. What if all those little houses were full of robbers? What if there were wolves in his backyard, or enormous snakes? And what if no one ever wanted to be his friend?

Now Stuart had something else to worry about. How was he going to get down?

Aunt Bubbles came outside. "Where is that boy?" she asked. "He should come in for lunch now." Her voice was very tiny.

"Up here!" Stuart shouted.

Aunt Bubbles looked all around. "My stars!" she screamed. "The clouds are talking!" She never thought the little speck in the sky was her nephew.

"All this excitement is making me hungry!" yelled Aunt Bubbles. "Too bad someone stole my angel food cake yesterday. It was lighter than air."

Yikes! Stuart thought. *It WAS lighter than air!*

"Run to the bakery! Get a pound cake!" he shouted. "A great big heavy one. Quick!"

Aunt Bubbles did. "Now what, clouds?"

"Cut the tires off the car," Stuart called down to her. "Tie them together to that split tree. Make a sling-shot."

"I understand, clouds!" shouted Aunt Bubbles. She fit the cake into the big slingshot. She pulled it back.

The pound cake shot up like a rocket. Stuart flew over and caught it.

ZiNG

Slowly, bite by bite, Stuart came back down. He landed softly on the roof. He ate the last crumb as he floated down the chimney.

"Oh, there you are!" said Stuart's mother. "We had quite a day! Aunt Bubbles cut the tires off the car. She thought the clouds were hungry."

"Too bad you missed it," said his father.

"Your parents were right," said Aunt Bubbles. "People *can* have adventures without capes!"

Stuart just smiled.

STUART GROWS TOAST

Stuart wanted toast. There wasn't any.

"Oh, rats," he said. "Toast is my favorite food."

He made a list.

Why I like Toast:

1) Warm
2) You can put stuff on it
3) Stays where you put it because it is not slimy
4) Smells good
5) Fits in your pocket

In your pocket! Stuart remembered! He was wearing his new cape! He checked the secret pocket. No toast. What kind of a cape was this? But wait . . . three seeds!

Stuart smiled. "Of course," he said. "Toast seeds." *That's* the kind of cape it was.

Stuart went outside. He planted the seeds in a nice sunny spot.

"What are you doing?" asked his parents.

"Growing toast," answered Stuart.

"You can't grow toast," said his parents. "Now good-bye. We're going to buy new tires for the car."

"What are you doing?" asked Aunt Bubbles.

"Growing toast," answered Stuart.

"Good idea," said Aunt Bubbles. "I'll make tea."

Stuart watered the seeds with melted butter. "OK," he said. "Now grow."

And they did. Three nice, big plants popped up at once. *Like toast from a toaster*, thought Stuart. At the tip of each plant was a little bundle of leaves.

Stuart peeled open the first green bundle. It was the size of his smallest fingernail. Inside was an even smaller piece of buttered toast!

Stuart tried to pluck it from the plant. But the tiny buttered toast was slippery. It slid out of his fingers and landed butter side down. It was ant food now.

But there were still two more plants.

And the bundles had grown! They were now the size of his hand! Stuart peeled open the second bundle.

Just then the mailman passed by. "My goodness!" he said. "What is that marvelous smell?"

"I grew toast," said Stuart. "Would you like some?"

Stuart picked the toast from the second plant. He gave it to the mailman.

"Delicious!" the mailman exclaimed. "That is the best toast I have ever tasted. Thank you so much! Now I must be on my way."

"You're welcome," said Stuart. "Good-bye."

Stuart turned to the third plant. The bundle had grown again! It was the size of his head!

How big could toast get? Stuart wondered.

The seeds had come from his new cape. Anything was possible.

Stuart squeezed his eyes shut. He waited and he waited.

While he waited, he worried. He had to go to school tomorrow. What if his number fives came out backward? What if he was the shortest kid in third grade? What if he didn't make a friend?

Worrying really was his best thing. Waiting really was his worst thing.

SCHOOL
TOMORROW
NO
friend
all
alone
SHORT
the
SHORTEST
in third
grade

Stuart opened his eyes. It was hard not to act surprised.

The last bundle was ENORMOUS!

He climbed up on a stump to peel back the leaves.

The toast inside smelled heavenly. It was warm and crunchy and perfectly buttered. And it was the size of a car! Well, a pretty flat car.

"Aunt Bubbles!" Stuart called. "Help!"

Together they dragged the enormous toast inside and brushed the grass off.

Stuart got a saw and sawed off some strips. They were as big as fence posts. "This is a lot of toast," he said. "Call the neighbors. Tell them to come to a toast party."

Everyone brought something to put on the toast strips. There was jam and jelly, of course. There was applesauce and cheddar cheese. There was strawberry yogurt and peanut butter and hamburgers. Someone brought hot fudge. One-Tooth hogged the tuna fish, but everyone else was good about sharing.

Sadly, none of the neighbors was going into the third grade.

But on the bright side, none of them seemed to be robbers. And none of them had noticed any wolves or enormous snakes hanging around the neighborhood.

Everything was delicious, and the toast stayed warm. Finally, when no one could eat another bite, the party was over.

"Good night, good night," the neighbors called. "We had a wonderful time!"

There was still a huge piece of toast left.

"Where are we going to put this?" Aunt Bubbles asked. "It's as big as a mattress."

Stuart smiled. He pulled out his list and crossed off number five.

Why I like Toast.

1) Warm

2) You can put stuff on it

3) Stays where you put it because it is not slimy

4) Smells good

5) Fits in your pocket

"These are all good things for a food to be. But they are also good things for a bed to be."

Aunt Bubbles helped Stuart push the toast into his room. They pushed his old, broken-by-the-dinosaur bed out the window. They piled quilts and pillows on his new toast bed.

"Lots of quilts," Stuart said. "I don't want crumbs."

Stuart was almost asleep when his parents came home.

"Good night, son," they said. "Are you warm enough?"

"Oh sure," said Stuart. "Warm as toast."

A BAD START

Stuart woke up worried. School really started tomorrow, but today was orientation day. A note had come. New students could visit a day early for orientation if they wanted to. It was kind of a practice day.

"What a good idea!" Stuart's mother had exclaimed. "An extra first day. You can get used to things!"

What a terrible idea, Stuart had thought. An extra

first day. Twice as many things could go wrong.

What if he did something stupid, and the other kids pointed at him and laughed? What if they laughed so hard they fell down on the playground? Then he'd never make any friends. Not after making everyone fall down on the playground.

Stuart flopped back down. His toast bed made a nice crunchy sound, but he couldn't enjoy it.

He was eight years old, and his life was ruined.

Then he sat up again.

Wait a minute. He had a cape! He'd probably have a really great adventure right in the middle of school! And all the kids would want to be his friend!

Stuart ran downstairs, starving. He slid into the kitchen, and his cape flapped out just right.

"Whoa, there!" his parents said at exactly the same time. "You can't wear your cape to school."

"I have to wear it every day," Stuart reminded them, pulling a jar of strawberry jam from the cupboard. "So adventures will happen. So the kids will want to be my friend."

Stuart's parents glared down at him with their no-argument looks.

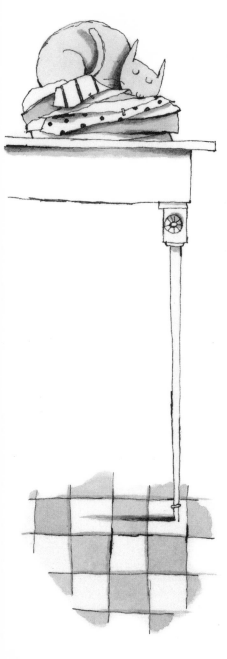

Luckily, Stuart had been practicing his own no-argument look in the mirror. This was a good time to try it out.

"Something in your eye?" asked his father, untying Stuart's cape.

"Do you have a stomachache?" asked his mother, folding it up.

Stuart grew weaker and weaker as he dragged himself across the kitchen to the table. He looked behind him to see if he was leaving a trail of melted bones.

His mother set his cape on the table. "There now, all ready for when you come home." One-Tooth curled up on the cape.

"Maybe that cape *is* magic!" laughed his father. "That maniac cat of yours is taking a nap, even though it's trash collection day!"

Tipping over trash cans was One-Tooth's favorite thing to do. Usually Stuart thought this was extremely funny, but today he moaned. He remembered what had happened on trash collection day last week. All his best stuff, gone.

"Eat your breakfast, Stuart," his mother said.

"You don't want to be late," his father said.

Stuart collapsed into his chair. How could his parents sound so cheerful? Hundreds of things could go wrong today. It was bad enough he didn't have a friend. Now he had to face it all without his cape.

Stuart tried to lift his toast. "Not . . . strong . . . enough . . ." he murmured. Even his tongue felt weak, but he licked a little strawberry jam off his toast. It tasted sad, like red glue, and it stuck in his throat.

"Good-bye, good-bye!" Stuart's family sang out the door. "Have a nice day!"

Stuart's father was going off to his job as a carpet cleaner. His mother was going off to her job at the beauty shop. Aunt Bubbles was going off to her job at the bakery.

None of them seemed to notice how dangerously weak he was.

"Mmff-hhmm," Stuart replied. "Glaaaaahhhhkkkk."

He was off to become a total flop as a third grader.

TRADING PLACES

Stuart was so weak he could barely walk. At the end of his street, he sat down on the sidewalk to rest. He watched a tiny ant crawl down into a crack in the sidewalk.

How he wished he could trade places with that ant!

He would just shrink down and disappear into that little crack. He'd build tunnels and eat cracker crumbs. So what if he didn't have a friend? All he'd have to

worry about would be not getting squished.

Of course, if he traded places with the ant, the ant would have to trade places with him. That's how trading places worked.

Stuart stretched out on the warm sidewalk to think about an ant going to orientation day.

A loud crash down the street ruined his daydream.

Stuart saw a garbage truck, he saw his cape, and he saw his cat.

"Stop, One-Tooth!" Stuart shouted.

One-Tooth's one tooth poked out of an enormous cat grin. She did not stop.

As One-Tooth backed up to ram into another bunch of trash cans, Stuart leaped onto the truck. He waded through all the trash and climbed up to the driver's seat.

"Move over," Stuart said firmly. He took the cape

off his cat. He put it around his own shoulders and took a deep breath of the good tie-and-magic smell. At this exact moment, he could feel all his strength rushing back to him. He knew what he had to do.

Luckily, driving was a lot easier than grown-ups pretended it was. One pedal to go, another to stop. Steer. But collecting the trash was a big job. Street after street, lined with trash cans. It took hours. At every stop, Stuart found something too good to throw away.

A curly wig, a box full of doorknobs, a bag of keys.

He put all these things up front with him. "Someone should do something with this great stuff," he said to his cat. "I wonder where the trash man is."

One-Tooth didn't answer. She was sound asleep, making a funny rattling sound. Exactly like snoring.

But only people snored, not cats.

And then Stuart realized a terrible thing.

Of course! One-Tooth had traded places with the

trash man! And if she had traded places with the trash

man, then that meant . . .

Stuart turned the truck around and tore back down

the street. He screeched to a stop at his house and

leaped down.

Curled up on the kitchen table was a man. His hat

said STANLEY, PUNBURY TRASH COLLECTOR, and he was

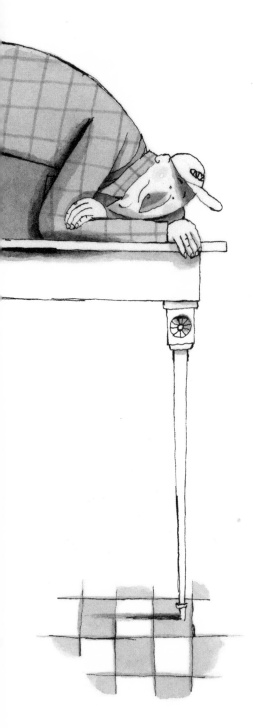

making a funny rumbling sound. Stuart wished it were snoring. But it sounded an awful lot like purring.

Gently, so as not to startle him, Stuart shook the trash man's shoulder.

The trash man yawned and stretched. He began to lick his wrist.

"Please don't do that!" Stuart cried.

The trash man blinked, and then rolled over onto his back.

Too late. Stanley, the Punbury trash collector, had turned into a cat.

Fleas. Hairballs. Raw mice for breakfast. And he, Stuart, was responsible for the mess. All because he had taken off his cape. He would spend the rest of his life in his room. Or in jail.

Unless he could change One-Tooth and Stanley back again.

Stuart grabbed a can of Kat Krunchees from the shelf, shook it, and headed outside. The trash man leaped off the table and followed, licking his lips. He followed Stuart right up onto the seat of his truck.

Stuart lifted his cat to the ground. One-Tooth took off after a squirrel. The trash man stared at Stuart as though he had never seen him before. It had worked.

"You were sleeping," Stuart explained. "Having a little catnap. Do you feel okay now?"

"Fine," answered Stanley. "But I can't nap. I have to do my work."

"Don't worry," Stuart told him. "It's all done. I collected all the trash in the neighborhood."

"Well, thank you," answered the trash man, sadly. "But that's not my work. That's just my job."

"Then what is your work?" Stuart asked, confused.

"I'll show you," the trash man said, pointing to an enormous barn at the end of the street.

Stanley drove Stuart to the barn and threw open the big doors.

Stuart had never felt so excited in his whole life. He trembled all over. Even his eyes were shaking slightly, but he could still see.

Row after row of tables piled high with neat stacks of useful things. Faucets, broomsticks, and broken TVs. Picture frames, bathtubs, and bicycle wheels. A saddle, a screen door, a chair without legs.

"People throw great stuff away all the time. They think it's junk, just because it's old, or broken a little. Maybe they don't see how great it could be. Maybe they're too busy to fix it. Anyway, saving it is my work. Too bad about today, now I'll never know what was out there. . . ."

"Wait!" Stuart shouted.

He showed the trash man all the great things he had saved.

"I can't believe it!" the trash man cried, wiping a tear from his eye. "Nobody else has ever understood. We can be partners in junk saving!"

Stuart and Stanley shook hands. They shared a snack of toast, and talked some more about trash. "Every day there's some new treasure in the trash," Stanley said. "And I never know what it will be. That's the best part."

"I know what you mean," Stuart answered. "It's like my cape. Every day something different happens. I never know what it will be. And that's the best part."

"Of course, saving junk is a big responsibility," Stanley said.

"My cape is a big responsibility, too," Stuart agreed. "I can't let anyone else wear it. I can never, ever, *ever* take it off."

Stuart knew he could explain this to his family. They liked the word *responsibility*. They used it a lot. He would always wear his cape, even when he went to —

"Yikes!" Stuart cried, jumping up. "School!"

Stanley gave him a ride to Punbury Elementary School, and Stuart raced inside to room 3B. No one was there except the teacher.

"Sorry I'm late!" he said. "The trash man turned into a cat, and I had to collect all the trash. But don't worry, I'm never going to take off my cape again!"

Mrs. Spindles stared at Stuart. "I think this is going to be an interesting year. But I'm sorry you didn't get to meet the other students. Maybe you could have made a friend."

Stuart smiled. That was exactly what he had just done.

STUART'S advice column

Don't leave anything good
outside on trash collection day.

If you're sharing food with
a ~~dinosor~~ dinosaur, take some
for yourself F I R S T.

There are no bathrooms in the sky.

Tuna fish and grape jelly don't taste
good together. (even on toast)

Try out your no-argument look on a
little kid F I R S T !